The Ghosts of Spiritwood

MARTINE NOËL-MAW

MARTINE NOËL-MAW

The Ghosts of Spiritwood

THE GHOSTS OF SPIRITWOOD
By Martine Noël-Maw
Originally published 2010 in French as
Les fantômes de Spiritwood
by Éditions de la nouvelle plume
Translated by the author

First English Edition
Published 2023 by Shadowpaw Press Reprise
Regina, Saskatchewan, Canada
www.shadowpawpress.com

Trade Paperback ISBN: 978-1-989398-62-3
Ebook ISBN: 978-1-989398-63-0

Cover and interior design by Edward Willett
English translation revised by Ingrid Alesich
English edition edited by Edward Willett

*In memory of my father, Marcel Noël,
my grandfather, Camil Lapointe,
Emma Larivière, and Ghislaine Giroux.
So many departed; so many sources of inspiration.*

MY STORY

I still have nightmares about the events that took place in that abandoned country school near Spiritwood. I'd seen disembodied spirits before but never like those.

My name is Ethan, and I'm seventeen years old. I've decided to write about what I went through earlier this year because, according to my mom, who's a psychologist, it should do me good.

We'll see.

It all started on a Friday. I was supposed to go camping with my class up near Spiritwood, in northern Saskatchewan, to watch the northern lights. It was Mario's idea. Mario's our teacher. I was about the only one in the group who'd seen northern lights before, during a fishing trip with my dad—the only trip we had ever made together.

Five of us didn't take the bus with the rest of the class because we had things to do in town. There was me, John and Reggie (the rival twin brothers), Britney, and Alex. (Alex's real name is Alexandra, but she hates it, so watch out if you call her that.) I'm good friends with Alex and John, but I couldn't care less about Reggie and Britney. Let's say we don't have too much in common. The only reason they were with us was I didn't have the guts to say no when they asked for a ride.

We left town late in the afternoon in my new car. I mean new as in "recently inherited," not as in brand-new. It was my mom's old car, a twelve-year-old four-door Corolla. A clunker, but it was better than being without wheels, like now.

We should have reached the campsite around eleven that night, but we never made it. So here's the detailed account of what happened to us near Spiritwood last June.

FRIDAY

We left Regina shortly after five. It was nice and hot, but the mood in the car wasn't good. I'd split the twins, seating John in the front and Reggie in the back, but it didn't stop Reggie from bugging his brother.

What else was new? Reg always finds a reason to hassle John. That time, it was about the soccer game he'd played the night before. One of the players from John's team had scored a goal in his own net. John's the goalie. And they lost 1-0 . . . it sucks, but you have to get over it.

Britney and Alex, two girls that have absolutely nothing in common, were in the back seat with Reggie.

It was around 10 p.m. when we drove through Spiritwood, a town of about a thousand people. A big sign on the edge of town announces, *Welcome to Spiritwood,*

Spirit of the North. North it is; they're right about that. The sun had set, but the sky was twilit.

A few kilometres past the town, a deer appeared right in front of us in the middle of the deserted road. I yanked the steering wheel to avoid hitting it and lost control. The car rolled over and ended up in the field. Thankfully, everyone was buckled up, and no one got hurt.

"What are you doing?" Reggie yelled as we hung there upside down. "You trying to kill us?"

"I didn't want to hit the deer!"

"What deer? I didn't see anything."

"John, did you see it?" I asked.

"No, I was sleeping. What a way to get woken up . . ."

"I saw it," Alex said. "It jumped right in front of the car."

I unbuckled, lowered myself to the ceiling, and got out of the car to check if I'd hit the deer. Once I got on the road, I looked around and saw no trace of it.

That's when I realized that my vision was blurred in my right eye. I'd lost a contact lens. It must have been somewhere in the car. *Might as well look for a flea on a football field,* I thought.

I returned to the car. The others were also out of the vehicle by then. Four of us—Britney preferred to watch— tried to put it back on its wheels, but we weren't able to. We needed a tow truck, but how can you get one north of the "Spirit of the North," where there's no cell coverage?

We were stuck, with no one on the road to help us. Since we had driven through Spiritwood a few minutes earlier, we decided to go back on foot. We left our luggage in the car, thinking we'd be returning soon, and off we went. I only took my backpack.

We headed south, and that's when I noticed a storm in the half-lit sky, coming our way. I picked up speed, walking in front of the others, my hands sunk deep into my pockets.

"Ethan, don't walk so fast," Britney said. "My feet hurt."

"We've been walking for less than ten minutes. If you can't keep up, you should go back to the car."

"No way! I'm not going back there alone in the dark."

"Anyone want to go with her?"

No answer.

"John? Reggie?"

The twins shook their heads. That surprised me because I would have guessed that Reggie would have jumped at the opportunity to be alone with Britney. He'd been after her for months.

"Alex, you want to go back to the car?"

"Why me? You want to get rid of the girls?"

"Calm down! If you don't want to go, you stay, that's all. The thing is, we don't know how far we are from Spiritwood, so . . ."

"Don't worry," Britney said. "I can walk even if it hurts. I'll do like I always do and shut up."

"That's a good one!" John said. "Since when are you able to stay quiet?"

"Since as long as you've said stupid things: since forever!" Reggie said.

"You're not going to start arguing again?" Alex complained.

"It's not my fault if he can't stop talking crap," Reggie said.

"You should shut your mouth instead of saying dumb things," John said.

"You want me to shut up?"

Reggie grabbed John by his collar. It's always like that with those two. Reggie thinks he's superior because he's ten minutes older. Ten minutes. Give me a break!

"Reg, leave him alone!" I said. "It's up to you: either shut up and follow or go back to the car. Understood? If we want to get to Spiritwood before the storm, we'd better hurry."

Reggie let go of John, and we resumed walking at a faster pace.

The approaching storm was straight ahead of us. Lightning flickered in the dark clouds and thunder rolled. We had to hurry! It's not a good idea to be in the middle of the bald prairie during a thunderstorm.

Britney's every step was accompanied by an "ouch!"

"What were you thinking, going camping in high heels?" Alex said.

"I imagine it may be hard for a tomboy to understand that real girls like to wear something other than Converse," Britney retorted.

"What did I just say?" I burst out. "I don't want to hear a word!"

I sounded authoritarian, but it was just a show. I really didn't like the situation we were in.

"How far do you think we are from Spiritwood?" John asked.

"I'd say about five or six K."

"You're crazy to want to walk all the way there," Britney said. "We're going to be attacked by bears."

"You're safe," Alex said. "No bear will touch you. They can't stomach high heels. Or gel nails."

I expected Britney to reply with something nasty, but she didn't say a word. I'd never seen her at a loss for insults before. Maybe it was because of the fact that even with Britney in high heels and her hair piled high, Alex was still way taller.

For three seconds, a huge flash of lightning illuminated everything like full daylight. That's when I noticed a fork in the road about thirty metres ahead of us. Then, the thunder rumbled, sounding like a big semi heading toward us.

"Did you see that?" Reggie asked. "There's a fork in the road. Which way should we go?"

"The way we came from," John said.

"Yeah! And which way is that, smart ass?"

John didn't reply.

"Which way should we go, Ethan?" Alex asked.

"Don't ask me. I've never been here before."

"You were driving."

"Yeah, but I didn't notice the fork."

It was true. I have to confess that I'd been on autopilot for the last few kilometres before the swerve. If I'd been concentrating on the road, I might have been able to avoid the deer without ending up in the ditch, and none of what followed would have happened.

"What does your gut tell you?" Alex asked.

"I don't know . . . I think that . . ."

"Let's go right," Britney said.

"Why right?" I asked.

"I've been in this area before. My uncle used to own a cabin nearby."

I was hesitant, but since she was the only one who knew the area at all, I decided we might as well follow her advice.

"Okay, let's go right, but we'd better hurry up before it starts raining," I said—a very small decision with big consequences. I adjusted my backpack on my shoulders, and we took off.

We went to the right, and shortly afterward, the surface of the road became bumpy. We stopped suddenly and stood close to each other in silence except for the intermittent electrostatic crackles of the storm and Britney's occasional squeak from pain.

Then the wind picked up. I searched the horizon, my eyes half-closed because of the dust, but I couldn't see the faintest glimmer of streetlights from Spiritwood.

"I'm starting to wonder if it was a good idea to leave on foot," John said.

"What else could we do, dummy?" Reggie said.

"We weren't going to spend the night in an upside-down car," Alex said. "There's nobody around."

"Anyway, I, for one, wouldn't have spent the night in the middle of a field," Britney said. "There are wolves and coyotes in this area, in case you don't know."

"Yes, but they're mostly interested in cows," Reggie said. "Er . . . I say that without a 'double entendre,' of course."

"Shut up and walk!" I said. Their chatter was getting on my nerves.

We walked a few more minutes before the rain started.

"We have to find shelter," I said. "Or at least get off the road if we don't want to get hit by lightning."

The storm was getting closer and closer, gaining in intensity. I saw a bush to my right. Another lightning flash revealed a building about fifty metres off the road in that direction. "Did you see that? There's a house over there."

"I don't see any lights," Britney says.

"Me neither, but there's a house. I saw it."

"I saw it, too," Alex said. "Let's go."

We left the road and ventured onto a dirt path narrowed by overgrown shrubs. *Whoever's living here doesn't take care of the pathway*, I said to myself.

All of a sudden, the storm broke. The wind became fiercer and raindrops started dancing on the ground, turning the path into a super-slippery river of mud. It was tough to keep going forward. John lost his footing and ended up in the mud on all fours. I would have laughed if I hadn't been afraid I'd end up in the same position. I helped him back to his feet.

It took us at least five minutes to reach what I thought was a farmhouse. In the pouring rain, I dug my flashlight out of my backpack to examine the building. All the windows were either boarded up or broken. The place was obviously abandoned.

"There's nobody here to help us," I shouted through the storm.

I noticed a plaque above the doorway: *1928*. Probably the year it was built.

"It's not a house," I yelled. "It looks like an old country school. An abandoned school."

"Who cares?" Britney said. "We can at least go inside and get out of the rain."

"Let's go," John said.

He was the first one to climb the half-broken steps. The door was locked tight with a chain and a rusted padlock, but the rain was getting inside through a broken window to the left of the door. We decided to do the same.

I scratched one of my arms on a piece of broken glass that was sticking out, but nothing serious. I was glad to get inside. We were completely drenched. I put my flashlight on the floor, so we could see something. We wrung out our clothes as best we could.

I was taken aback when I saw Britney's face. Her mascara was smeared around her eyes and down her cheeks. "You should see your face. You look like a raccoon!"

We all laughed except for her.

"Very funny. You're just a bunch of jerks." She tried to wipe off her face, mumbling.

I picked up my flashlight and swept it around the room. Two big blackboards on the walls confirmed it was, in fact, an old school—a one-classroom school. A few desks were piled up in a corner. Right beside them, an old mattress rested on the floor in front of an armoire with its door half-open. There was nothing in it.

Next to that was a door. I went to check where it led,

pointing my flashlight at the floor because it was covered with rubbish: pages from burst books, empty beer bottles, and cans were scattered everywhere. I shined my light through the doorway. It led to the basement. I had a peek down the stairs. The total darkness sent a shiver down my spine.

"It looks like party central," John said, pushing a bottle with his foot.

"It's disgusting," Britney said. "We can't stay here."

"If you prefer to be out in the storm, don't let us hold you back," I said.

"Watch the way you talk to her," Reggie warned me.

"She should be like us and put up with it."

"It's true; it's not very inviting," Alex said.

"Okay, it's not the Hotel Sask, but it's better than sleeping outside."

"You don't expect us to *sleep* in here," Britney said.

"You have a better suggestion?"

"No, but . . ."

"We'll clean up a spot, sit on the floor, and wait for the storm to move on."

John and I kicked away the papers, bottles, and other junk with our feet and tossed them in a corner. Once we were done, I turned off my flashlight.

"What are you doing?" Britney asked. "Turn that back on. Now!"

"No way. We have to spare the batteries."

"I told you to turn it back on!"

"Calm down. Your eyes will get used to the darkness before long."

"I can't stand . . . I . . . I am. . ."

"There's no reason to panic. Nobody is going to attack us here. Especially in this kind of weather."

Honestly, I said that not only to reassure her but also to reassure myself.

Britney calmed down, and we all sat in a circle in the half-light. It was still pouring rain, and a cold wind was coming in through the broken windows.

Almost immediately, a bluish light came on. It was Britney's cell phone.

"There's no reception, but it's bright," she said.

"You should save the battery," I said.

"What for? You think a cell tower is going to pop up overnight?"

Britney put the phone down in front of her. We remained quiet. As soon as the light turned off, Britney touched the phone, and it came back on—again and again.

"It reminds me of a game we used to play when we were little," John said. "You remember, Reg?"

Reggie shrugged his shoulders, staring at the phone.

John carried on. "Our dad had a watch that lit up in the dark. We couldn't read time back then, but sometimes, when we went to bed, we'd take it with us and play with it."

"You took it to bed because you were afraid of ghosts," Reggie said.

"It's not true. I've never been scared of ghosts."

"Liar!"

"It's true!"

"Whatever," Alex murmured. "I was scared by a ghost once. A real one."

We all looked at her, waiting to hear more. She made us wait.

"Go ahead!" John said after a while.

Alex shrugged. She leaned back and looked at the ceiling. "It happened five years ago. I'd just turned twelve. I was playing Scrabble with Steph in my room. She was staying over for the night. It was late. We should have been in bed, but it was too hot to sleep. What happened that night made me change my mind about ghosts. Before, I didn't believe in them."

"What happened?" I asked.

"My grandfather came to say goodbye."

"Your grandpa came to say goodbye," Reggie said. "That's a super terrifying story. . ."

"Let me continue. My grandfather came to say goodbye. . . the night he died."

Alex's last words remained suspended in the air. I believed her because I know that ghosts do exist.

"It's impossible," Britney said.

"I'd say the same thing if I hadn't had this experience," Alex said.

"What happened?" I asked. "Tell us."

"We were playing Scrabble on the floor when we heard a voice calling me from downstairs. 'Alexandra!' It was a man's voice."

"Your dad?" Reggie said.

"That's what Steph thought because she heard the voice, too. 'Your dad's calling you,' she said, but my dad was in Ottawa. There was only Steph, my mom, and me in the house, and my mom was asleep in her room. I know because we could hear her snoring. So we resumed playing as if nothing had happened. A moment later, we heard the call again, 'Alexandra!' Steph said that my dad must have come home. I started to get scared because I knew he wouldn't have come back unexpectedly like that. And it wasn't my dad's voice anyway."

"Whose voice was it?" John asked.

"Stop it!" Britney said. "I don't want to hear this kind of story."

"Don't tell me you believe in ghosts?" Reggie said.

"I don't believe in them, but I don't like this kind of story!"

"Use earplugs," John said.

"I was petrified," Alex continued. "I didn't dare go downstairs to check. We tried to keep playing, but I couldn't concentrate. My mind was focusing on the stairs, right in front of my bedroom door, which was wide open. Then a bit later, we heard the voice calling me again. I checked the time. It was 1:36 a.m.

"Steph said, 'Well, Alex, we're not crazy. There's someone calling you downstairs.'

"'Who could it be?' I said.

"'I don't know,' she said. 'Go and check!'

"I got up and walked out of the room. I was so scared I was afraid I'd wet myself. I went down the stairs as slowly as possible to avoid making noise. Ethan, you've been to my place; you know that everything squeaks in our old house."

"It's true."

"I got to the living room, and there was no one there. When I got to the front room, I checked the door. It was locked. I looked outside and didn't see anything unusual. Then I went to the kitchen to check the back door. It was locked, too. I turned on the outdoor light and saw no one outside.

"I ran back upstairs. Steph was waiting for me at the top of the stairs. I told her that there was nobody there. 'That's impossible!' she said. 'There must be someone.' I swore to her there was no one."

"What happened next?" John asked.

"Well, not long after that, we heard the voice calling my name again."

"Shut up! You're gonna give me nightmares!" Britney whined, pressing her hands against her ears.

"Who wants to go to sleep? Whoooooo?" John said, waving his hands.

"Stop being silly!" Reggie said.

"Shh! Let her continue," I said.

"When we heard the voice again, we both jumped into my bed, and I turned the light off. We were back to back. Steph was facing the wall. Then we started hearing footsteps coming up the stairs."

"Shut up, please!" Britney pleaded.

"Don't worry," Reggie said to her. "It's just nonsense."

He put one arm around Britney's shoulders, but she moved away. "I don't like this story. Alex, please, stop."

"Brit!" John pleaded. "She can't leave us hanging like that. Alex, continue."

"Sorry, Brit. I'm almost done, but the scariest part is still to come, so . . ."

"Listen to some music," I suggested.

She pulled her earphones out of her bag, planted them in her ears, plugged them into her phone, and started a playlist loud enough not to hear what was coming.

"So, we heard footsteps on the stairs. The fourteen steps creaked one after the other. Then, all of a sudden, the temperature dropped in the room. We were suffocating, and a second later, it was cold. That's when I felt a presence . . . I still shiver when I think about it. I could have screamed, called for my mom, but I was paralyzed by fear. I felt the presence move inside the room. It was getting closer to the bed. It's weird, but the closer it got, the less scared I was. And then, at one point, I felt totally relaxed."

"Did you see anything?" I asked.

"No. Nothing."

"Then how can you tell the presence was getting closer?" John asked.

"It's a sensation I had, a magnetism that I felt. When the presence got to my bedside, it stopped. Then nothing happened for a few seconds, but I could feel it right there, in front of me. After that, and this is the most bizarre part, the presence sat down. A heavy mass sat down on the edge of my bed."

"That can't be!" Reggie said.

"I swear to God! The mattress pushed down, and I rolled forward."

"You must have been so scared," John said.

"No, that's the thing. I wasn't scared at all anymore. I was calm. I could feel it was a benevolent presence."

"How?" John asked.

"It was just a feeling. Then I heard a voice. With my ears or in my head, I'm not sure. It said to me, 'I came to say goodbye, but mainly to tell you never to worry in life. I will always look after you.' As I heard that, I felt a hand caressing my hair. He didn't say his name, and I didn't see him, but I knew it was my grandfather. My father's father. It lasted a few seconds, and then, he was gone."

"If this happened to me, I would wet my pants," John said.

"I thought nothing could scare you," Reggie said.

"What happened next?" I asked.

"Nothing. I fell asleep."

"Did you know then that your grandpa was dead?" John asked.

"No, and that's the most interesting part. When I got up the next morning, my mom was on the phone in the kitchen. She was talking to my dad in tears. She said, 'It happened during the night. Your mom tried to wake him up this morning and . . .' I knew who she was talking about. My grandfather died of a heart attack during the night."

"Wow! What a crazy story," John said.

"Have you seen his ghost since?" I asked.

"No. And Steph and I never talked about it, except once. Last year, I asked her if she remembered the night my grandfather had passed away, and she said, 'Yes, and I don't want to talk about it.' It did happen. It wasn't a dream."

"Are you done?" Britney shouted.

Alex nodded, and Britney removed the earphones. "What do we do now?" she asked.

We all looked at her.

"What?" she said.

"What's there to do, you think?" Alex asked.

"I don't know . . ."

What was there to do except wait for the storm to end?

"When my grandmother died, she stayed with us." The words came out of my mouth by themselves. I had never shared that experience with anybody other than my mom, who never believed me.

They all stared at me with surprised looks on their faces. A flash of lightning lit up the inside of the school, and the thunder boomed nearby.

"Explain yourself," Alex said.

"You're not starting again," Britney complained.

"We're not starting again; we're continuing," John said.

Britney put the earphones back on.

I was hesitant to share my experience, but I went ahead. They could call me crazy if they wanted to.

"I was three years old when my grandmother died. I was very young, but I do remember. At the funeral home, my mom lifted me up so I could see Granny in her coffin. I touched her face. It was so cold. I'll never forget that sensation. When we left, I asked my mom when I was going to see Granny again. She replied that I would never see her again, but she was dead wrong."

"How so?" Alex asked.

"Shortly after her passing, I began seeing a shadow on my bedroom wall at the foot of my bed. It would appear as soon as I'd lie down. It scared me at first, but I soon understood that it was my grandmother."

"How did you know?" John asked.

"I felt it like Alex said. What I saw was the shadow of a skinny body. My grandmother was tall and very skinny. The way I saw her, she was, like, sitting at the foot of my bed, and a light was sculpting her shadow against the wall. Except there was no light."

"Not even a nightlight?" Alex asked.

"Nope. I never had a nightlight. What fascinated me about this apparition was the fact that it was moving. She would have her hands resting in her lap and then cross her arms or turn sideways."

"Did she speak to you?" Alex asked.

"She did communicate with me, but not with words. It was always very soothing. The first couple of times, I went to fetch my mom. 'Come see Granny! She's in my room!' I'd tell her.

"'That's impossible,' she'd say. 'Your granny is dead.'

"Every time I'd get back to my room with my mom, the shadow was gone. So I quit mentioning it to her."

"Did those visits last for a while?" John asked.

"Oh, yeah! The whole time we lived in that apartment on Victoria Street. I was thirteen when we moved, and Granny was still there the last night."

"You're claiming you saw your grandma's ghost in your room for ten years?" Reggie said. "You're sick in the head!"

"Did you take pictures?" John asked.

"No. It never crossed my mind. I just enjoyed her presence. She didn't come every night, but mainly when I had had a rough day, when I'd been pushed around at school . . ."

"You?" John said. "The best-built football player? You've been pushed around at school?"

"You're the tallest and the strongest one," Alex said. "It's hard to believe."

"I may be the tallest, but it doesn't matter. Some people will always find a reason to push someone around. Anyway! When I wasn't feeling well, my granny was there for me."

One case, in particular, came to mind. "I must have been ten. My mom was completing her degree in psychology, and money was scarce. She'd bought me a Roughriders jersey at Value Village. It looked new except for a small tear on the shoulder. I was so happy I didn't wait for her to fix it before wearing it.

"The next day, Tom Vezina cornered me at school. He put his finger in the tear and said out loud, 'Hey, poor slob!'

"I told him I was neither poor nor a slob.

"'Yes, you're poor because you're wearing my old rag,' he said. 'That hole, right here? I made it. My mom gave it to Value Village. That's where you shop for clothes, so you're poor.' He said that in front of everybody in the gym, and he started laughing. I was so ashamed.

"I went straight back home and cut the jersey into pieces with a pair of scissors. That night, my granny's ghost spent a long time at the foot of my bed."

We kept talking until late into the night. The storm eventually stopped, and we fell asleep, one after the other. Britney was snoring, with the earphones planted in her ears. The music was still playing.

Alex's body was pressed against mine. I could feel her breath on my back.

Too bad she has a crush on John, I thought.

DURING THE NIGHT

I was the first one to wake up. It was quiet in the school. The rain had stopped. My right arm was so numb that it took me a while to be able to move it. As I sat up to massage it, I accidentally kicked Alex.

She woke up with a start. "Hey? What's going on?"

"Nothing, it's only me. Sorry."

"What are you doing here? Where am I?"

"In the abandoned school. Remember?"

"What school?" She rubbed her eyes, sat up straight, and looked around. "Oh, yeah, I remember. What time is it?"

I turned on my flashlight to check my watch.

"Twenty after two."

"A.M.?"

"Of course, what do you think? It's dark out."

"Not really. Check."

I turned toward the window and, wow! The clouds were gone, and a curtain of green light was hanging in the sky. I'd never seen anything like it. "That's awesome!"

Someone moved. It was Reggie.

Then John woke up, too. "What's going on?" he asked in a husky voice.

"Have a look outside," Alex said.

"Oh, wow!"

I got up. Alex and John, too. Reggie leaned over Britney and removed her earphones. The music was still playing.

"Brit, wake up," he said. "Come see the sky."

"What? No more ghost stories!"

"No, better than that. Come and see."

Britney got up to join Reggie and us in front of one of the broken windows.

"*Aurora borealis*," I said. "Named after . . ." I was trying to remember what I'd learned in my research. "Oh yeah! *Aurora* for the Roman goddess of dawn, and *borealis* for Boreas, the . . ."

"The god of the north wind," interrupted Reggie. "We know. You're not the only one that has done the research." He elbowed John.

"Hey! Don't push me!"

"Stop it, you twins!" Alex snapped. "You should enjoy the show instead of squabbling."

"At least we didn't come all the way up here for nothing," Britney said.

She took pictures of the sky with her phone until the battery died.

The northern lights were absolutely spectacular. They looked like gigantic sails hanging in the deep blackness, blowing in the wind. It was the ideal moment to tell the others about the legend I'd found while researching.

"Do you know the legend of the northern lights?"

No one did.

"I found it on the internet. According to the legend, the northern lights are the spirits of deceased people who . . ."

"Not another ghost story!" Britney cried out.

"Yeah, sorry. Put your hands on your ears."

Instead, she leaned the top part of her body out the window to get a better view.

"So, as I was saying, according to the legend, the northern lights are the spirits of deceased people who want to communicate with the living."

They all turned toward me.

"It's a bit short for a legend," Alex said.

"That's not all. When we see northern lights, we can establish contact with the spirits by whistling."

"Whistling?" Reggie said.

"Yeah, whistling."

"So, what you're saying is that if we were to whistle,

right now, right here," John said, "we could make contact with the dead?"

"Stop talking about that," Britney said. "It doesn't make any sense."

"Why are you scared, then?" John asked.

"I'm not scared!"

"You're shaking! I can see it."

"I'm shaking because I'm cold, dummy!"

I grabbed my backpack to fetch a special object I had brought to do an experiment. "Look at this." I showed them a thing that looked like a giant ladybug.

"What's that?" Reggie asked.

"It's a whistle to call the good spirits."

"You believe in those stupid stories?" Reggie asked.

"Whether I believe or not is irrelevant. I can test the legend either way."

"Where did you get that?" Alex asked.

"I bought it at Wanuskewin."

"It's an aboriginal legend?" John asked.

"I believe so. I read it, and then, two days later, when we visited Wanuskewin, I found that whistle in the gift shop. Quite a coincidence, eh?"

"You don't have the guts to blow it," Reggie said.

I placed my fingers on the holes on the top and bottom of the instrument. The others were looking at me. I felt stupid and excited at the same time.

Reggie challenged me again. "You don't have the guts."

"Don't tease him, Reg," John said. "He could do it."

"So? He blows the whistle, and then what?" Reggie said, pushing John. "You think some ghosts are going to appear? You believe that, twit?"

"Oh, we know you, Reg," Alex said. "You only believe in what you can see and touch."

"That's not true. Take you, for example. I see you, and I believe you exist even though there's no way I'd touch you. Ha! Ha! Ha!"

"Everybody knows you prefer Barbie dolls," John said, looking at Britney.

"You moron!" Reggie said, slapping the back of John's head.

"Ouch! That hurt!"

"Reg, leave him alone!" Alex pleaded.

"He's not even worth getting my hand dirty," Reggie said. "Okay, Ethan, are you gonna blow that whistle or not?"

"Nothing bad can happen," Alex said.

I thought she didn't sound very convincing—or convinced.

I was hesitant even though I knew I was going to do it. I looked at the sky. The colour of the northern lights had faded. I took a deep breath, raised the whistle to my mouth, and blew.

A high-pitched sound came out of the small instrument made of terracotta. I modulated it by moving my fingers as one does with a recorder. The northern lights started dancing in the sky. I felt like a snake charmer.

"Stop!" Alex said.

I quit. I was out of breath anyway.

Silence didn't come back right away. The notes continued to travel in the cool night air. I felt a bit dizzy.

"Don't stop!" Reggie said. "Keep going!"

"No!" Alex said. "We shouldn't fool around with that kind of stuff."

"You're just a coward! You sound like my grandma. 'Don't tempt the devil.' Pfft!"

"Have you ever had a supernatural experience?" Alex asked.

"Never! Because I am sane."

"Me, too! And I guarantee you that it's a bad idea to fool around with the afterlife."

Alex was right. I should have refrained from blowing the whistle. I put it in my pocket and moved away from the window. I didn't feel too good all of a sudden. "I'm going to lie down."

Alex and John followed me.

"That's it, go back to sleep, wusses," Reggie said.

Britney joined us.

Standing in front of the window, Reggie put two fingers into his mouth and started whistling.

I had a restless sleep. And I wasn't the only one. The hard floor, the cold drafts, and the lack of blankets all contributed to the discomfort of our makeshift shelter. Some were snoring while others mumbled incomprehensible jargon.

At one point, I woke myself up with my own snoring. I was on the verge of going back to sleep when I heard a dog bark.

So, we're not that far away from civilization, I thought. Judging by the high-pitched sound, it hadn't come from the type of dog one would normally keep on a farm, such as a German shepherd, but rather from a hysterical small dog, the kind a lady might carry around in a purse. It lasted a few seconds, and then, nothing. I fell asleep.

A bit later, I was awakened again by a voice. Someone was calling me. "Ethan!"

I jumped and looked around. From what I could see through the darkness, everybody else was asleep.

I closed my eyes and heard the voice again.

"Ethan!"

It sounded like a child's voice. A boy. I sat up.

"Ethan!"

"What is it?" Alex murmured.

She'd startled me. "You hear that?" I asked.

"Yeah. Someone's calling you. Who is it?"

"I don't know."

The others were still asleep. I turned on my flashlight and checked around but didn't notice anything.

"It sounded like it came from the back of the room," Alex said. "From the armoire, maybe?"

"Or the basement."

"What's that voice?" John asked.

"You heard it, too?"

"Yeah, and I don't like it. It's not one of us."

I immediately thought of Alex's story about her grandfather. Was someone coming to say goodbye to me?

"What time is it?" John asked.

I consulted my watch. "Almost three-thirty."

The three of us sat still, in silence. Everything was quiet. Suddenly, the night felt like it would never end. I promised myself that when all this was over, I would go to church. It's crazy, I know, but that's what went through my mind.

Then the mysterious voice resounded once more.

"Ethan!"

"It isn't from the basement," Alex said.

I looked at the back of the room. The armoire door was still ajar.

"It sounds like it's coming from the cupboard," John said. "Why don't we check it out?"

"Are you crazy?" Alex blurted.

"What's going on?" Britney asked. "What are you up to?"

"Nothing," John said. "Go back to sleep."

"That's easy to say. I'm sore all over. And I'm freezing," she said as she sat up.

Reggie woke up, too. I told him about the voice we'd heard.

"It must be the voice of your conscience, suffocating in your little head."

"Very funny . . ."

Minutes went by, and I was about to fall asleep again when Alex squeezed my arm and motioned me to look at the back of the room. What I saw gave me goosebumps.

The cupboard door was slowly opening, and a dim light was shining from the inside. Then, all of a sudden, a small, luminous shape came out of it. It stopped in mid-air before moving toward the stairs leading to the basement and disappeared.

Incredulous, I turned toward Alex. "You saw that?"

Stunned, she nodded. The others turned around to see what was going on, but it was too late.

Right after that, a foul odour spread inside the school. It was like a mix of algae and rotten eggs. Anyway, it stank!

Britney was the first one to complain about it. "Ugh! Who farted? Is it you, John? Did you eat a rotting carcass, or what?"

"No way! It must be Reg. Hey, Reg?"

"It's not me."

I hesitated before speaking. "He's right. It's not him. I think we're dealing with something else."

"Like what?" Reggie asked. "What could stink that bad?"

"It's unbearable!" Britney said. "I'm going to throw up."

She got up and stuck her head out the window to get some fresh air, and we all joined her.

"I never smelled anything that gross," Alex said.

"We have," Britney said. "Whenever you wear perfume."

Being on the verge of puking didn't stop her from hurling venom. She and Reg laughed.

Alex ignored them. I have to say, Alex has always been well-armoured against nastiness. Even when she was little, kids would make fun of her because of her red hair and freckles. On top of that, she was the tallest one at school—everything she needed to get unwanted attention. Before starting Grade 9, she transformed and became Alex, sporting a pixy haircut, a pierced nose, and black clothes. I never told her that I missed Alexandra.

The stench faded a bit.

"If none of us launched a stink bomb, what was it?" Reggie asked.

"I don't want to scare anyone," I said, "but I think we're dealing with a ghost."

"Shut up!" Britney shouted. "You're talking nonsense."

"Ethan's right," Alex said. "I saw it, too."

"You saw what?" John asked.

"A ghost. We saw a ghost coming out of the closet and heading downstairs."

"You're sick in the head!" Britney said.

We remained silent for a while, and the foul odour eventually went away completely. We sat down again.

"We should try to call it," John suggested.

"Call who, dummy?" Reggie asked. "Our phones don't work here."

John let the insult go.

In my opinion, Reggie constantly belittles him out of jealousy because John is a real chick magnet. When he walks into a room, the girls stop and stare. They're crazy for him.

"I meant we should try to call the spirit," John said.

"Didn't we already call it with the whistle?" I said.

"I mean, we should try to make it talk."

"Yes!" Alex said. "Let's make it talk."

"Make a spirit talk?" Reggie said. "You're nuts, all right! Tell me how you do that?"

"You can make fun of it, but it's possible," Alex said. "Last summer, at camp, me and three other girls held a séance one night."

"What kind of a séance?" Britney asked.

"A séance to make spirits talk."

"That's rubbish," Britney said.

"Let her blab. She believes it," Reggie said.

Alex ignored them and carried on. "We met in the cafeteria after everyone else had gone to bed. In the afternoon, we'd cut out the alphabet in cardboard letters and a *Yes* and a *No*, to create a sort of spirit board. We lined up the twenty-eight pieces on the table, put a cup upside down in front of them, and started asking questions."

"What questions did you ask?" John said.

"They asked the spirits about your IQ, and the answer was zero," Reggie said.

"Very funny," Alex said. "We started by asking if there was a spirit present and if it wanted to communicate with us. We all had a finger touching the cup. At the beginning, nothing happened. We repeated the question many times before it started moving.

"What moved?" Britney asked.

"Duh! The cup! You don't know that game?"

She shook her head.

"You ask questions, and the spirits answer by pointing either *Yes* or *No*, or by spelling words."

"Why would anyone want to communicate with spirits anyway?" Britney asked.

"Just for fun!"

"I don't see what's fun about it."

"Let her tell her story," John said.

"Finally, when we asked yet again if a spirit wanted to communicate with us, the cup moved slowly and stopped in front of *Yes*."

"You did it. You made it move," Reggie said. "Everybody knows that."

"I was there, and I can assure you that none of us pushed the cup."

"We should try it," I said.

"We don't have anything to make the letters," John said.

I thought for a moment. "I know! We can use that paper scattered on the floor. We tear it to bits and write letters on them."

"Using what?" John said. "Does anyone have a pen?"

Nope. But I had another idea. "Brit, you must have some makeup in your bag. I don't know what you call it . . . the pencil crayon you put around your eyes."

"It's a kohl pencil, dummy, not a crayon."

"Yeah!" exclaimed John. "A pencil or a lipstick."

"If you think I'm going to waste my makeup on your stupid game . . ."

"Come on, Brit. Be cool for once," Alex pleaded.

We managed to convince Britney. She pulled two pencils and three tubes of coloured gloss from her bag. Ten minutes later, we had twenty-eight pieces of paper from old books. I laid them in a semi-circle on the teacher's ancient wooden desk, which we pulled from underneath the mountain of pupils' tables, and I put the *Yes* to the left and the *No* to the right.

"John, pass me an empty bottle, will you? We'll use it as a pointer."

He handed me a bottle, and I placed it in front of the semi-circle.

"Ready?"

No. Britney had to "go." Since there was no toilet in the classroom, she asked Alex to go outside with her. When they came back, I asked again. "Ready?"

No objection this time. I was excited and nervous. What was I expecting? Certainly not what happened.

"Okay, let's begin."

"Don't count on me because I have no desire to see any spirit," Britney said.

"It's not about seeing spirits," I said. "We just want to check if there are any in the school."

"What's the difference?" she asked.

"The difference is that we're not asking them to show themselves. We just want to know if they're here and if so ask them who they are and *why* they're here. Let's take a few seconds to concentrate."

"Concentrate on what?" Reggie asked.

"Concentrate on . . . I don't know. Just empty your mind."

"Won't be hard to do for my bro," Reggie said.

John breathed through his nose and closed his eyes.

After a few seconds of silence, I started the séance. "Okay, everybody. Let's touch the bottom of the bottle. Not to move it, but just to transfer some energy."

"I'm not touching it," Britney said, crossing her arms.

"Your choice."

The rest of us slightly touched the bottle, and I asked the first question, using a deep, low voice. "Spiriiiiit, are you heeeere?"

"Seriously?" Reggie laughed. "You sound like a rotten actor in a rotten movie. If there are no spirits, who's gonna answer no? Duh! "

"Shut up! Leave it to him," Alex whispered.

Reg was right, so I rephrased my question and took a different tone. "Is there a spirit in the room?"

Silence.

I waited a bit before repeating the question. "Is there a spirit in the room?"

The tension was palpable. We were all staring at the bottle.

All of a sudden, a draft of freezing air swept across us.

"Is there a spirit in the room?"

As soon as I finished asking the question, the bottle moved slightly to the left. My heart started pounding, and I was trembling. The bottle was really moving on its own! And then it stopped, pointing directly at *Yes*.

"This can't be," Reggie said.

I was struggling to remain calm. My jaws were

clenched. *What do I do now? What question do you ask a spirit?*

John came to the rescue. "Did you die here, in this school?" he asked.

Slowly but steadily, the bottle did a 180-degree turn to the right, pointing at *No*.

I was really impressed. I still had no idea what other question to ask.

Alex jumped in. "Are you a woman?"

The bottle didn't move.

"Are you a man?"

The bottle turned in the opposite direction and pointed to *Yes*.

"It's a man," Alex whispered. "What's your name? Can you spell it for us?"

The bottle moved toward the right about thirty degrees and stopped, pointing at a letter.

"J," Alex said. "Britney, can you write it down?"

Britney took one of her kohl pencils and wrote the letter in the palm of her hand. Straight away, the bottle moved and stopped in front of a second letter.

"O."

And a third.

"S."

And a fourth one.

"H."

And then nothing.

"Josh," Britney read.

"Yeah. A man whose name is, or was, Josh. What are you doing here?"

The bottle didn't move.

"Your question is too complicated," I said.

"Go ahead, then," Alex said.

I'd thought of another question. "Do you need help?"

As soon as I finished my sentence, the bottle twisted toward the *Yes* so fast that it startled us.

"Wow! You saw that?" I asked.

"I bet you did it," Reggie said.

"Not at all! It moved on its own."

"What do we ask now?" Alex whispered. "What we can do for him?"

"First, let's question him on his identity," I said. "His age, for example."

"Shoot! We forgot to make numbers," John said.

"No big deal. He can spell it out."

"Let's hope he's not ninety-nine years old 'cause it could take a while," Reggie said.

"Very funny," I said. "How old are you? Can you spell out your age, please?"

"Why are you so polite? It's just a spirit," Reggie said.

"So what? Excuse him," I said to the spirit. "Can you spell out your age?"

The bottle moved to the right and pointed at the letter

N. Then it pointed at the I. After that, it went back to the N.

"N, I, N," I whispered. "Nine . . . not nine, I hope. Not a child!"

The bottle moved to the left, stopped on the E, and then nothing.

"We're dealing with the spirit of a child," Alex murmured.

"Stop!" Britney shouted. "I can't stand this stupid game."

"It's not a stupid game," I said. "And we can't stop now. He needs our help."

"You're scaring me with your spooky game!"

Honestly, I didn't feel too brave either.

"What do we do now?" Alex asked.

"Let's ask him what he wants from us," I said. "What can we do for you?"

Suddenly, the bottle started spinning around like the needle of a compass gone nuts. It spun and spun dozens of times. Britney started crying, and Reggie hugged her.

"That's not normal," John said. "It should . . ."

"You bet it's not normal," interrupted Reggie. "You are talking to a *spirit*! Hello?"

The bottle eventually stopped spinning. I wasn't at ease with what had just happened. I moved away from the desk. "I've heard it's dangerous to do this kind of thing because we could open a portal without knowing what kind of spirit we might attract."

As I said that, I heard an unpleasant, high-pitched squeak. I turned toward the blackboard and saw letters forming in the half-light. I turned on my flashlight.

You've heard the expression "hair standing on end"? It's possible, believe me. I'm sure we all had our hair standing straight up as we watched what was appearing right before our eyes:

GET OUT!

Then it stopped. How did those words appear? I looked around and didn't see any chalk. Why would Josh want us to leave when he'd just asked for help? It didn't make sense.

"Maybe the words were already there when we got here, but we didn't notice," John suggested.

"No. I would have seen them when I walked around the room. These letters just appeared. You all saw that, right, like me?"

Speechless, they all nodded very slowly, their eyes glued to the board.

Then, out of the corner of my eye, I saw a desk leap at least a metre toward us.

"You saw that?" I yelped.

"Yes, and I really don't like it," John said.

"Me neither," Alex added. "Josh, is that you?"

No answer.

"What's going on?" Britney said. She sounded scared.

"They're playing stupid tricks, that's what's going on," Reggie said. "Let's get out of here."

"It is, like, four in the morning, and the rain has started again," Alex said. "Where could we go?"

"The sun will come up soon," I said. "Let's just stay awake."

"I have an idea," Alex said. She took out her phone. "Let's do what they do in the paranormal TV shows."

"Those shows are staged," Britney said.

"You can think whatever you want," Alex replied. "But in those shows, they often record voices."

"You mean EVP?" I said. "Electronic voice phenomenon?"

"Yes. If we record with a digital device, we can hear voices that we can't normally hear because the frequency is too low."

"How does it work?" John asked.

"We ask questions and leave some time for the spirit to respond. Then we play the recording to listen to the answers."

"You're so gullible!" Reggie said. "Brit is right. These shows are staged. It's impossible."

"You're really stupid if you believe in that kind of hocus-pocus," Britney said.

She was playing tough, but I could have sworn she was on the brink of crying.

"Let's try it," John said.

Alex nodded. "Okay, everybody, be quiet. Don't say a word. Promise?"

We remained silent. The only noise was from the rain falling on the roof. Alex motioned us to sit on the floor in a circle, and we followed her instructions. She put the phone in the middle of the circle and tapped the record button.

"You should say something to make sure it's recording," John said.

"You just did. Thanks. Is there anyone in this room?"

"Of course, dum-dum! There are five of us," Reggie answered.

"Reg, shut up, please. Is there a spirit in the room?"

Alex waited a few seconds before asking another question.

"Why are you here?"

A few more seconds went by in silence.

"Can we do something for you?"

A few more seconds of silence.

"What else can I ask?" Alex murmured.

I had a question. "How did you die?"

The second I uttered those words, a noise started—a tapping against the floor. I turned on my flashlight and saw, at the other end of the room, a desk rising and falling very fast. *Tap! Tap! Tap! Tap! Tap!* The noise was constant.

Alex stopped the recorder, and the desk quit tapping. "What do you think of that?" she asked.

"Seems to me that someone is protesting our recording," John said.

"Seems to me that you think we're idiots," Reggie said.

"Looks like someone doesn't like us asking questions," I said. "Let's play the recording."

Alex pressed play. We could hear a light background noise. Probably the rain. Then John, Alex, and Reggie's comments, and then Alex's first question. "Is there a spirit in the room?"

The silence that followed was interrupted by a muffled sound as if someone was talking through a tin can. A single syllable. A "yes," maybe?

The recording continued. "Why are you here?"

A voice a bit clearer said a word hard to hear. "Bur . . ."

"Burble?" I said.

"Burden?" John said.

"Buried?" Alex said.

We kept listening. "Can we do something for you?"

Straight away, a resounding "Yes!" came out of the device. I got goosebumps.

Then, as soon as the question, "How did you die?" was asked, the voice started saying something, but another voice, or a groan, rather, covered it up.

Then we heard the desk tapping . . .

The squeaking noise started again, but this sound was live. I pointed my flashlight at the board. Once again, in front of our eyes, we saw words forming. The same ones.

"I'm fed up with your little scheme!" Britney said. "You are so not funny that I'm not going to wait for sunrise to leave." She got up and grabbed her bag. "Reg, you're coming with me?"

Reggie didn't move.

"Are you coming with me or staying with these idiots?"

"Brit, wait," he said hesitantly.

It was obvious he didn't want to leave. I jumped in. "Wait a bit, Brit. It's going to be bright out soon. You can't go anywhere now. We don't even know where we are or which way Spiritwood is."

"There must be some indications somewhere."

"Of course there are, and we'll be able to see them as soon as the sun is up."

Since Reggie wasn't showing any desire to follow her, Britney sat down and gave him a disgusted look that he pretended not to notice.

"What do we do now?" Alex asked.

No suggestions. I think we were in shock. The accident and all the rest were a lot to take in for one night. And the thought of the presence of a spirit in distress was bothering me.

"We can't pretend not to know that a spirit needs help," I said.

Silence.

"John?"

"I'm thinking."

"Alex?"

"I agree with you. We can't ignore it."

Then, something extraordinary happened in the silent classroom. The bluish light that Alex and I had seen earlier reappeared. The foul odour came back, too, but not as strong as the first time. Thank goodness!

The light was shining up the staircase. It was coming toward us!

Britney asked what we were staring at. She didn't seem to be able to see it. Or Reggie, either.

As the light approached us, it got more intense, forming an orb with vaporous contours.

"Reg, what are they doing?" Britney asked.

"No idea. Looks like they're mesmerized by something. Or they're just plain crazy."

The luminous ball was about the size of a volleyball. It was floating one metre above the floor, between us and the blackboard.

I'm not exactly sure how to describe the phenomenon, but some kind of intelligence, or rather, some sort of consciousness, seemed to emanate from the ball. I immediately thought it was Josh's spirit, that he had concentrated his energy to communicate with us in a more direct manner. Not knowing whether he wanted us to help him or to leave, I was perplexed.

"Look," I said softly. "You see in the centre? It looks like there's a core."

"Yeah," Alex said.

"What can it be?" John asked.

No one knew the answer. After being immobile for a while, the orb moved closer to the blackboard. That's when we started seeing images inside it. It was like they were revealed against the opacity of the board. Fascinated, I stood up and got closer.

"Careful, Ethan!" John warned me. "We don't know what it could do."

"My feeling is that it's a positive energy. Josh, is that you?"

The bluish light turned silvery.

"It's him," Alex said. "Josh, tell us what happened to you."

Then, the orb fused with the blackboard, creating a sort of screen on which an image appeared that we couldn't identify at first. Slowly but surely, the blurred lines became sharper, and the shape of a human body appeared: a child holding something in his arms. A dog.

I focused on the child's face. The boy had hollowed cheeks and sported a crew cut. His big eyes looked terribly sad. I was deeply moved. He opened his mouth and contracted his face like he was screaming. Was he calling for help? Ordering us to leave? There was no sound. My voice trembled as I attempted to talk to him. "Is that you, Josh?"

He nodded.

"Do you want us to help you or to leave?"

He became agitated. We saw his lips forming words inaudible in the land of the living. Then, little by little, I understood without hearing. He was communicating with ideas instead of words, like my grandmother and Alex's grandfather.

Find me.

"'Find me,'" I repeated in a low voice. "You want us to find you? What is it . . . you want to play hide and seek?"

He took on an even more sombre look and shook his head from left to right.

"No," Alex said. "He doesn't want to play hide and seek. Never again hide and seek."

"He doesn't seem to like that game," John said.

I don't know where the idea came from, but I proposed a hypothesis. "Maybe he had an accident while playing hide and seek. Is that it, Josh?"

He nodded up and down so fast that the image became blurry. The dog he was holding started barking. It was the same bark that had woken me up earlier. When Josh stopped nodding, his expression was even sadder and more imploring than before.

"What happened to you? How did you die?" Alex asked.

He articulated some syllables on his mute lips, and I caught the words "fell" and "stream."

"You fell in a stream?"

Yessss!

I immediately understood. Or so I thought.

"You fell in a stream while playing hide and seek?"

Yessss!

"And your body hasn't been found? That's why you're asking us to find you. Is that it?"

Yessss! Find me!

At that moment, the same desk that had been tapping earlier started doing it again. *Tap! Tap! Tap! Tap! Tap!* And then, it flew across the classroom. I had to duck to avoid being hit by it.

It smashed against the blackboard, right where Josh was. The image disappeared.

Britney burst into tears. Reggie held her close.

"What invisible force could have done that?" Alex asked.

"I don't understand," I said. "It's certainly not Josh."

"Maybe it's the same entity that wrote 'Get out!' on the board," John suggested.

"Yeah, the same one that interfered during the recording," Alex added.

"You're right," I said. "There must be another entity in here. Who could it be?"

"I don't know, but it's aggressive," Alex said.

We waited a bit, and nothing else happened. I decided to call out.

"Who's here besides Josh?"

"Shut up!" Reggie said. "What's gotten into you? Why are you scaring Britney like that? What did she do to you? You won't get away with it!

I decided not to waste my time arguing with him and repeated my question. "Who's here besides Josh?"

Silence.

"What should we do?" John asked.

"You think you're being smart with your tricks," Reggie said.

"Shut up!" John retorted.

I had never heard John talk to Reggie that way. Him either, I think, judging by the look on his face.

I kept trying to reconnect with Josh. After a couple of minutes, a misty light appeared, but almost immediately, an object hit the blackboard, and the light faded away.

The object in question was my flashlight. It ended up on the floor, shattered into small pieces.

It was almost dawn. I had to come up with a plan to help Josh. Because I was determined to help him.

"I won't leave this school until I've tried everything I can to appease the spirit of this child," I announced.

"I'm thinking the same," Alex said. "We can't abandon him now that we know, but we don't have much info to conduct a search."

"She's right," John said. "All we know is that he fell in a stream, but which stream? Where?"

"Let's be logical," I said. "If Josh's spirit is linked to the school, it's because the place matters to him. We could think that he liked it a lot or that he died here, but he mentioned a stream, so it seems clear to me that it should be close to the school. No?"

"It makes sense," Alex said.

"You're a bunch of lunatics," Reggie said. "You see and hear things that don't even exist."

"You're pretending just to scare me," Britney said.

I looked at Alex and John. Was it possible that Reg and Brit hadn't seen or heard anything? I was about to ask them when Reg got up.

"Come on, Brit! They had enough fun at our expense. Let's go."

"No, stay!" I said.

"No way!" Britney said.

"If you leave, you're going to bungle everything," Alex said.

"Bungle what?" Reggie asked. "You're just making fun of us."

"That's not true," I said. "You don't understand. Since we didn't show up at the campground, they must be looking for us."

"I certainly hope so," Britney cried.

"Don't go!" I pleaded. "If the police find you, they'll come and get us, and we won't be able to help Josh."

"Ethan, listen!" Reggie said, two centimetres from my nose. "Your playacting was very funny, but enough is enough. You wanted to scare us? Well done! Now, we're getting the heck out of here. Adios!"

And they left.

SATURDAY MORNING

It took me a while to go back to sleep after Britney and Reggie left because I was worried. I was concerned that they'd tell the police, or whoever found them, where we were. If anyone came to get us, we'd have no choice but to leave, and I didn't want to go before having a chance to try to help Josh.

It was bright outside when I woke up. My first impression was that the classroom had lost its aura of mystery, even though I knew that supernatural events had actually happened during the night.

Alex and John were up already. I was surprised and relieved to see that the deserters had come back. Britney and Reggie were sleeping side by side a couple of metres from me. When they woke up, they explained they'd come back because they couldn't agree on which direction to take.

We shared the energy bars and the bottle of water I had in my backpack. Two bars divided by five is not what I call a feast, but it's better than nothing.

While we were eating, I noticed that Britney was staring at me. "Why are you looking at me like that?"

"How come one of your eyes is blue, and the other one is brown?"

Shoot! I'd forgotten I'd lost a contact lens. She *would* have to notice it. It was rather embarrassing.

"It's nothing. I lost a lens last night."

"What's the deal?" Reggie asked. "Are your eyes blue or brown?"

"Brown."

"I get called Barbie, but it's the football player that wears coloured lenses," Britney said. "Ha! Now we've seen it all!"

"Do many players change their eye colour like that?" Reggie asked. "Do you do it to see the football better or to seduce your opponents?"

"Forget it."

"What else about you is fake?" Reggie asked. "Come on! It's confession time."

"Reg, stop," John said.

"No. We have the right to know. Come on! What else?"

"Forget it," I repeated. "It's just a detail."

"We thought you were an authentic dude," Britney said.

"*You're* talking about authenticity?" Alex said. "That's a bit rich!"

"Your blond hair, is that artificial too?" Reggie asked.

"No, that's my real colour."

"Whoa!" Britney said. "You won't make me believe that. Your stylist had a hand in it. Admit it."

"Leave him alone," Alex said.

"What about your muscles?" Reggie asked. "I bet they're blown up by steroids."

"No! I've worked hard to get them. I won't let anyone accuse me of using drugs."

"Our sportsman just went from authentic to synthetic," Reggie said.

"He went from blue-eyed charmer to brown-eyed liar," Britney said.

"Enough!" Alex said.

It was embarrassing that Alex came to my defence, but I was unable to stand up for myself even though they were a real pain. I'm like that. I want to save others, but I can't fight for myself outside a football field.

When Brit and Reg were done making fun of me, it was time to go look for Josh's body. Not having a map or compass, we had to rely on our instinct. If there was a stream nearby, it should be relatively easy to find. We just had to look for groves since trees grow more by the waterside.

I picked up my backpack. "Shall we go?"

Alex and John got up. John's pants were caked with dried mud. "I'll wash the dirt off once we've found the stream," he said.

Britney and Reggie remained seated on the floor. I stood in front of them. "Get up. What are you waiting for?"

Britney looked at Reggie.

"Ethan, we're not going with you," he said. "We're going to Spiritwood."

"Don't do that. If you don't want to come with us, fine, but stay here."

"No way," Britney said as she got up with her purse under her arm.

"Brit, stay! Please." I would have begged her on my knees.

"Wait for us here," Alex said. "We're going to do a search, and we'll come back. Reg, tell her to stay."

He got up and whispered something in Britney's ear.

"Well, okay," she said. "We'll wait for you."

I was relieved. How gullible could I be?

We found the stream in no time. Or rather, we found *a* stream. We had no way of knowing if it was the right one. We spent a lot of time walking alongside it, searching the bushes for any trace of human remains.

I wrote that like it's the most trivial thing in the world. "What did you do today?" "Oh, not much. We looked for a child's body." "Sounds like fun."

Nonetheless, I wonder what we'd have done had we found a cadaver in broad daylight. Would it have been more or less frightening than what happened next? Hard to say.

We walked on one side of the stream for some time, then we crossed it and walked on the other side on the way back. We'd gone quite far from the school. In the end, we didn't find anything except for some animal carcasses, a fox and two deer among them.

We got back to the school late in the afternoon, empty-handed, hungry, and covered in mosquito bites. What little repellent I had hadn't been enough for the three of us.

When we got back, the classroom was empty. No trace of Reggie or Britney. John found a note scribbled with one of Brit's makeup pencils.

You can go to hell with your crazy stories! B & R

"I knew we couldn't trust them," John said as he ripped the note. "Let's go find them."

"Not so fast!" I said.

"Why?"

"I suggest we stay here another night."

"What? Are you nuts?" Alex said.

"We have nothing to eat," John said. "Nothing to drink."

"I have a bag of nuts, and I refilled my water bottle at the spring."

"For sure, Reg and Brit will return with someone to get us," Alex said.

"We can hide."

"Where?" John asked.

"Well . . . in the basement. Let's go check while it's still bright out."

"I don't feel like it at all," Alex said.

"Come on. Let's go see. Who knows what we can find there?"

"Not food, that's for sure," John said.

Before going downstairs, I checked inside the armoire. It was empty except for a bell—like the ones you see in old movies that the teacher swings up and down to herd the kids to school—and an abacus.

Alex stood by the doorway to the basement. "You're coming?" she asked.

"Madam changed her mind? Good! John, you stay here in case Brit and Reg return?"

"No problem. I'd rather stay up here."

I wasn't scared to go downstairs, but I took the bell with me just in case. It was heavy enough to knock someone senseless if necessary. I held it by the clapper to avoid making noise.

The staircase was very narrow. I went down first, and Alex followed me closely. Visibility was good because the sun was low and shining through the basement windows.

The air got cooler as we got lower. There was an earthy odour. It smelled like the potato cellar on my grandfather's farm. The basement was the same size as the classroom.

"Hey, look!" Alex exclaimed. "There are some restrooms."

There were indeed two restrooms at the back, to my left, one for boys and one for girls. In one corner sat a broken ping-pong table and a sandbag game board.

"Must have been the game room," Alex said.

I put the bell on top of a pile of boxes. There was a water tank at the far end of the basement. It was used to collect rainwater, as I learned later when researching country schools (by the way, I found a very interesting site: www.virtualmuseum.ca). And right in the middle of the room stood an old furnace, a wood-burning antique, it looked like—there was a pile of wood in a box right next to it. I was about to have a closer look when I heard John's call.

"Hey! The police are coming!"

"What?"

"There's an RCMP cruiser coming up the drive."

It was out of the question for me to leave. I shouted at John, "Come on down! Come and hide!"

He flew down the stairs. "They stopped the car half-way, and they're coming on foot. Reg and Brit are with them."

"Those two couldn't keep their mouths shut!"

"Ethan, why are you getting so upset?" Alex said. "What's the problem?"

"What's the problem? You want us to be forced to go back to Regina now?"

"I think we should, yes! Otherwise, we're going to be in trouble."

"We're already in trouble! One more night won't change anything."

"He's not wrong," John said.

"Alex, you'd be willing to abandon this after what we went through last night? Knowing now what we know about Josh? We'd have gone through all this for nothing!"

"I'm not saying we should abandon the search. We'll just have to come back another time."

"Come back? This is a five-hour drive from Regina! I won't be able to come back before fall. I'm going to spend the summer with my dad in Winnipeg."

"This is no time for discussion," John said.

"Alex, if you want to leave, go, but don't tell them we're here."

I ran into the boys' restroom, hoping that Alex would stay. John came in behind me. We heard footsteps upstairs and then voices. A few seconds later, someone came down the stairs.

An unknown voice, strong and full of authority, called our names. "Ethan? John? Alex? Are you here?"

I heard a second person coming down the stairs. I ran into a stall and climbed on the toilet seat while John hid behind the door. Right away, a policeman pushed the door open and called our names again.

"Ethan? John? Alex?"

He turned on his flashlight and checked the room. The stall I was in didn't have a door. I was sure the cop would see me.

The light beam swept across the room, and I caught a glimpse of my fragmented reflection in the broken mirror. *Oh, my God!* I scared myself. My heart was thumping so hard I thought it was going to leap out of my chest.

After an infinitely long moment, the policeman closed the door. I'm sure John was as nervous as I was.

The police went into the girls' room, calling for us. It took a while, but they eventually went back upstairs. What a relief! I'd never been that tense in my entire life.

They chatted upstairs for a while, and then it fell silent. John climbed up the stairs on the sly to check if they were gone and called out a few seconds later, "The coast is clear!"

The girl's restroom door opened, and Alex came out. She had stayed. I was so glad I could have hugged her.

Did I mention that I really like her?

SATURDAY EVENING

It had been a close call. After we went back up to the
classroom, John stationed himself in front of the
window to be on the lookout in case the police returned. I
shared my bag of nuts with him and Alex. It was still
bright outside. With a few hours to kill, we chatted.

That night, I learned that Alex is quite knowledgeable
about the paranormal. She explained to us, among other
things, that there are different kinds of ghosts.

"There are the ones that specialists call the
pranksters. They are often the ghosts of children who get
a kick out of hiding things. For instance, one morning, I
couldn't find the socks that I'd just put beside my bed. I
looked everywhere, two, three times—I couldn't find
them. I even stripped my bed. Nothing! They'd
vanished. I took another pair out of my dresser, turned

around, and what did I see? My socks! Laid out on my bed, side by side, on top of the bedding that I'd just tossed around."

"You're joking," John said.

"Not at all! It happened last summer. The day my cousin Christine died."

"Do you think she did it?" I asked.

"I can't prove it, but you'll admit that it's a heck of a coincidence. Especially since she was quite a prankster."

"She was the best," John said.

"Getting back to the different kinds of ghosts," Alex said, "there are also those who are after revenge, for one reason or another, and those who don't know they're dead."

"How can somebody not know they're dead?" John asked.

"Apparently, it happens mainly in cases of sudden death," Alex said. "There are also entities who deliberately remain attached to the world of the living because they've committed a crime and are afraid to be exposed. And then there are ghosts on a mission, like to right a wrong or make a truth known."

"What kind of ghost would Josh be?" John asked.

"I think he's on a mission. He wants his body to be found, probably to get a proper burial and bring closure to his family."

"I hadn't thought about his family," I said. "It must be

a living hell for his parents. I wonder how long he's been missing?"

"Maybe a year, two years, or even more. And they don't know what happened to their son," John said. "Like you said, it must be hell."

"Thinking about his parents makes me want to help him even more," I said.

"I'm glad I stayed," Alex said.

"What I don't understand are the interferences that happened last night," John said.

"Remember what we said. There may be another entity involved," Alex said.

"Yeah."

"I'd say that this entity doesn't want Josh's body to be found."

"Maybe," I said. "They both have a reason to remain here: Josh wants his body to be recovered, and the other one wants to prevent this from happening. It's our task to find out why."

"I'm thinking the same," Alex said.

"It's disturbing to think someone could both be dead and still remain here," John said. "When I die, I hope I go somewhere else. I certainly don't want to get stuck in a school . . . Brrrr!" He changed the subject. "So, why do ghosts manifest themselves only at night?"

"You're sure of that?" Alex said. "They may manifest

themselves during the day, too, but we don't notice because there's too much energy of all kinds in the air."

"Personally, I've never seen anything in broad daylight," John said. "Or at night, either. Except for last night."

"I've seen one manifestation during the day," Alex said. "It involved my other grandfather, the one who died when I was ten. It happened last winter. I was home alone. I was preparing a snack in the kitchen when, all of a sudden, I heard a big noise. Like glass breaking and empty cans clattering. A heck of a racket! It was coming from the basement. I got so scared that I didn't go downstairs right away to check. When I finally took a peek, the only thing I saw was a broom at the bottom of the stairs. No broken glass, no cans. And that broom I saw is kept at the *top* of the stairs, beside the recycling bin that's placed *behind* the door to the basement."

"How did it end up at the bottom of the stairs?" I asked.

"It's a mystery. I went down the stairs to pick it up, and as I got there, I got a whiff of Aqua Velva."

"A whiff of what?" John asked.

"Aqua Velva. You know, the cheap aftershave. As soon as I smelled it, I thought of my grandfather because that's what he used. We always gave him some for Christmas. When my mom came home, I asked her what date he'd been born. It was that day. I'm convinced it was a sign from him. Besides, he'd been a janitor all his life, so the broom was right up his alley."

"You interpreted this as a message from him?" John asked.

"Yes. It was his birthday, and he manifested himself, so I'd think of him."

"Come on!" John said. "You really think that's possible?"

"Absolutely. It's like, if you start thinking about someone who's passed, it could mean that he or she needs prayers."

"That's a weird idea," John said. "Do you pray?"

"Of course. Not every day, but I do."

"That's stupid," John said.

"Not at all!" I said. "I read an article in one of my mom's psychology magazines about an experiment they've conducted on prayer. A group of people prayed for patients who were about to undergo surgery, and they healed faster and with fewer complications than the ones from the control group who didn't get prayed for."

"I believe that," Alex said. "The human brain is very powerful. We can heal ourselves or make ourselves sick with our thoughts. Prayer and autosuggestion work."

"That's a bit much," John said.

"What she says is true. If you focus on something, positive or negative, chances are it will materialize."

"For example," Alex said, "if you constantly think that

bad stuff will happen to you, that you're going to fail or whatever, chances are it will happen because that's where you direct your attention, your energy."

"John, remember what our driving instructor used to tell us? 'Don't look at the ditch, or you'll end up in it. Focus on the road because that's where you want to be.'"

"Does this mean that last night you were looking at the ditch?" John asked.

"Ha! Maybe," Alex said. "Your attention was definitely on the wrong thing."

Embarrassingly, I couldn't argue with that.

"I read something about Mother Teresa," Alex went on. "One day she received an invitation to participate in a demonstration against war, and she declined, saying, 'Come back when you plan an event promoting peace.'"

We chatted until dark. I must admit I felt less and less brave the more I learned about phenomena similar to the ones we'd been through the night before.

We were hoping to see more northern lights, and we weren't disappointed. These were even more spectacular than the previous night's. They formed a gigantic pink curtain in the middle of the starry sky.

"Let's go, Ethan, blow your whistle," John said.

I took my whistle, stuck my head through the window, and blew.

"Not so loud!" Alex said. "What if the police were still in the area?"

"Shoot! You're right. I didn't think about that."

I blew the whistle for a mere couple of seconds, but apparently, the spirits were paying attention because, right away, my phone started ringing.

"What's that music?" Alex asked.

"It's my phone."

"It can't be," John said. "There's no coverage here."

Not only that, I knew my phone was turned off. Intrigued, I grabbed my backpack and searched for my phone. I thought it might be my mom. She was going to give me an earful. *Maybe better if I don't answer,* I thought.

I found the device and checked the display. I almost dropped the phone when I saw who was calling.

I showed it to the others. "Check this!"

Alex and John opened their mouths when they saw who it was.

"It's him!" John exclaimed.

"Josh? That's impossible!" Alex said.

"Impossible is the word. Especially since it's not even turned on."

"Answer it!" John said.

"Do it!" Alex said.

I pressed the hands-free button. "Hello?"

All we heard was electrostatic noise.

"Speak louder," John told me.

"HELLO?"

"Help me . . ."

The voice was faint and distant, the voice of a frightened child.

"Who is it? Who's calling?"

"It's Josh . . . Help me. Find me."

"We're willing to help you, Josh, but we need more information. We searched along the stream all day and didn't find anything."

"I'm not near the stream."

"But you told us that . . ."

"I'm NOT near the stream."

"Where are you?"

"I'm here!"

It felt like an electrical shock went through my entire body. We all stared at each other with panicked looks. There was a cadaver in the school? I didn't know what to say or think.

"Ethan!"

"Yes, Josh. I'm still here."

"You have to search in the . . ."

All of a sudden, my phone became burning hot. I dropped it, the call ended, and it shut off.

"Why did you throw it?" John asked.

"It burned my hand!"

"You're being silly."

"No, I'm not!" To prove him wrong, I grabbed his arm with my still-hot hand.

"Ouch! Let go of my arm, it's burning!"

"You see? I'm not joking."

"There's definitely an entity trying to prevent Josh from communicating with us," Alex said. "He said we should look in . . ."

"In what?" John asked.

"In the . . . in the . . ." I was trying to think of something.

"In the armoire?" John said.

"No, we already looked," Alex said.

"In the . . . in the basement?" I said.

"In the basement?" Alex repeated.

"Yes, in the basement!"

Alex made a funny noise. She sounded like a puppy that doesn't want to go outside in the winter. It was obvious she didn't want to go back down there. Me either, by the way.

I offered a solution. "What if we wait till tomorrow morning?"

"I suppose we could," John said. "But we'll have to be quick and early in case the police come back. And I'm really looking forward to going back home."

"Yeah, a shower and a good meal would be great."

"Okay, guys. It's settled. We'll wait till morning," Alex said.

Still shaken by what had happened, we sat down and discussed our summer plans to clear our minds before trying to sleep.

I was relieved that the evening ended without any other supernatural phenomena, but my relief was short-lived.

SATURDAY NIGHT

I woke up in the middle of the night with a very unpleasant feeling. It was like someone was breathing down my neck. A breath that made me shiver.

I put my hand on my neck, thinking it must have been a draft coming through the window, then realized that, *No, dummy, you're facing the window!*

I turned in a flash, and that's when I saw it.

You know the word "bloodcurdling"? That's exactly what happened to me. It was like my whole body froze instantly. I was facing a ghostly figure straight from my worst horrific nightmares. About the same size as me, the thing was kneeling, bent forward, staring at me with teeth bared in a horrible grin. I quivered as I felt its icy breath on my face. Its protruding eyes with no pupils were animal-like. Its skin was cracked like an old piece of dead wood.

Its hair looked like it was covered in frost, with its bangs combed down into a V-shape.

What's one to do when facing such a monster? He wasn't there to bring me flowers, I knew that for sure!

I had no means of defending myself. I was paralyzed with fear. Believe me, it can happen.

Ideas started bumping into each other in my head at 200 kilometres per hour. The worst imaginable scenarios popped into my mind. I pictured myself hung by the feet from one of the ceiling's beams, my eyes ripped out; news headlines across the country saying, *Three teens savagely slaughtered in an abandoned school near Spiritwood*; my poor mother, unable to overcome her grief, committing suicide. A concentrated dose of anxiety and horror was sweeping through my mind when the ghost spoke to me.

"Get out! Leave!"

"Who are you? What do you want?"

I was out of breath, my throat was dry, and my whole body was shaking.

"Get out! Go away and never come back!"

"Not before we find Josh's body."

"I'm telling you to get *ouuuuuuuuut!*"

"No, you get out!"

Where did I get the nerve to defy him? That remains a mystery, but I'd managed to make him angry. He grabbed my neck and proceeded to strangle me. John and Alex woke up.

"Ethan, what's going on?" Alex asked.

I couldn't speak. I couldn't breathe.

"Ethan, what's the matter?" John asked.

What was the matter? I was being strangled by a ghost, and my friends couldn't see it!

"Is he epileptic?" John asked Alex.

"Not that I know of."

"He's convulsing. We've gotta do something!"

"Maybe he's swallowing his tongue. That's why he has his hands around his neck."

"Grab his left arm; I'll grab the right one," John said.

They struggled to get my hands away from my neck while I was struggling to slacken the ghost's grip. The three of them were against me! I was close to fainting. I felt incredibly lonely. I was sure I was about to die.

"Ethan! Ethan! Come back," Alex called.

"Ethan, you'll be fine, buddy."

It was impossible for me to communicate. The ghost would not let go of me. My last hour had come.

I don't know how long it lasted, but finally, the ghost released my neck and turned toward John.

"Ethan, are you okay?" Alex asked.

"What happened to you?" John said.

I couldn't utter a sound. My throat had been crushed. I was coughing. It was very painful. I looked at the ghost and pointed at it in an attempt to draw John's and Alex's attention to the entity, but they didn't get it.

"He's trying to tell us something," Alex said. "Ethan, what's wrong?"

At that point, the ghost transformed itself into a ball of grey light that dissolved against John like a cloud of smoke. The moment that happened, I saw John's appearance change in the rays of moonlight that dimly lit the room. John, who always stood as straight as the athlete that he is, hunched over. Then, he spread his legs, put his fists on his hips, and stared at me. A sombre stare. An evil stare. My friend was no longer in control of his body. We were in real danger.

I was coughing and coughing, incapable of catching my breath. I was sweating like a pig despite the nearly freezing temperature in the room. That monster had crushed my larynx and vocal cords. Alex was kneeling beside me.

"You're going to be okay, Ethan. You're going to be okay," she kept repeating, one hand resting on my shoulder. Although I was shaking my head, she kept saying I'd be okay.

John slowly came closer to us. He looked at me lying on the floor like I was some despicable vermin. Then he smiled, kicked me in the ribs, and screamed: "GET OUT!"

"John!" Alex cried out. "What are you doing?"

"You too, snooper, get out!"

"What's the matter with you?"

He kicked me again.

"Stop! Are you crazy?" Alex shouted.

She stood between us. John grabbed her by the shoulders and threw her against the wall.

I had to regain control of my faculties. My football player instinct kicked in. I got up and tackled John right in the stomach, and he fell backward.

Panicking, not understanding what was happening, Alex was screaming at the top of her lungs. I had to explain the situation to her, so I screamed louder than her.

"Alex, it's not John! It's not him!"

"What do you mean?"

"A bad spirit took possession of him."

"What?"

"It tried to strangle me, and then it took possession of John."

"Josh's spirit?"

"No, another one. An evil one!"

"Let's get out of here!" Alex said.

"We can't leave John like that."

"What are we going to do?"

"I have a bungee cord in my bag. Give it to me."

John sat up.

"Hurry up, Alex!"

"I can't find it."

John got to his feet.

"It's bright yellow. You can't miss it!"

"Got it!"

John started toward me just as she threw the cord at me. I quickly made a slipknot—not an easy task when you're shaking all over. My plan was to tie John's wrists, so he couldn't hit us. Then, I was going to try to tie his ankles. I'd seen a cowboy do that at a rodeo during Agribition, but it was with a calf, not with a raging, mad spirit.

"Come on, cutie, come closer," I said. Anything to try to give myself courage. I had never needed some so badly.

"Leave! Get out of here and never come back," John muttered, coming closer one slow step at a time.

"What if we do what he wants?" Alex suggested.

"And abandon John?"

"If you go, I'll leave your friend alone," the entity said.

"How could I trust you? You tried to kill me."

He was very close to me. I threw the cord and caught his left wrist. He yanked it, and I lost hold. He was too strong for me. At that point, the only solution that came to mind was to run away.

Then Alex started talking to him. "You're the one interfering when Josh communicates with us."

"If you've got a problem with that, then get the hell out of here!"

He looked disgusting. He was spitting as he talked, and froth was running down his chin.

"Who are you?" I asked.

"I'm the guardian of this place, and I order you to leave."

"Not before you leave John's body," Alex said.

"Don't wait till my patience runs out." He cracked the cord like a whip and hit Alex right in the face. She screamed.

"Alex, are you okay?"

"It's burning! I think he sliced my cheek!"

"Move away!" I said.

She moved against the wall behind me, and I turned my attention back to the thing that had taken over John's body. "What did you do to Josh?"

"I protected him."

"Protected him against what?"

"Against snoopers like you."

"Tell us who you are, and we'll leave."

"Liar! You have no intention of leaving."

I don't know if he could read my mind or if that was just a lucky guess. "Okay. If you know that, you should also know that we won't leave until we find Josh's body."

"He's mine, and he's gonna stay here! Get out of this school!"

All the rubbish that was on the floor started floating around the room.

"I said GET OUT!"

"Did you have anything to do with Josh's death?" Alex asked from behind me.

"That's none of your business."

"Yes, it is!" I said. "He asked us for help."

"You can't help him."

"Yes, we can!"

In a flash, John was two centimetres in front of me, roaring like a beast: a penetrating, guttural growl that made me shudder. I felt such intense cold and horror that my heart skipped a few beats. I fell backward like a plank. Alex threw herself at John and started hitting him with her clenched fists.

"No, Alex, don't do that! Run away!"

I was paralyzed. All the muscles in my body were as stiff as a corpse. Everything was swirling around me. I saw Alex lifting in the air with no one touching her. She started screaming.

And then, another scream covered Alex's. "Toby, no! Toby! Stop!"

I recognized Josh's voice. Right after that, the stuff stopped floating in the air, Alex fell on the floor, and I was able to move. I went to Alex and helped her get back on her feet. There was blood running down her cheek from where the bungee cord had hit her.

"Toby, stop tormenting them," Josh said.

"Shut up and go away!"

I looked around but couldn't see the kid. "Josh, where are you? And who's Toby?"

"It's me!" John shouted in a husky voice. "And I forbid you to say my name."

I don't know what got into her, but Alex started chanting his name. "Toby! Toby! Toby!"

"Stop! Are you crazy?" I said.

"No, if we manage to make him fly off the handle, maybe he'll leave John's body."

It was a gamble, but I started repeating his name too. "Toby! Toby! Toby!"

"SHUT UP!"

He hit the blackboard with his fist so hard the slate cracked.

"Toby, leave John's body and let them take mine away," Josh pleaded.

"Never!"

"Why are you so adamant about keeping him here?" I asked.

He shut his eyes, maybe in an effort to contain his anger. He was about to blow up

At that precise moment, Josh's spirit appeared in front of the board beside John. Like the night before, he was wearing a windbreaker and holding a small dog. "I died because of Toby. He pushed me into the stream."

"You were *pushed* into the stream?" Alex said. "You didn't fall?"

Josh shook his head, and his dog barked.

"Is that true, Toby? You pushed him?" I asked.

John unclenched his fists, and the tension gradually left his face. Beads of sweat stood out on his forehead. "It was an accident."

His voice was so faint I wasn't sure I'd heard right.

"Tell us what happened," Alex said.

He shook his head, but we had reached a turning point. Within a few seconds, he let his guard down. He started to weep. It was bizarre. I had never seen John cry.

"Tell them what you've done," Josh said.

Toby kept shaking his head.

Josh started crying, too. I didn't know that ghosts could cry. "Admit that you pushed me into the stream."

Toby grabbed his head with both hands. "I didn't want that to happen. I didn't. It was just a game."

"A game that went very wrong," Josh said. "Tell them what you did."

Toby wiped his face. Or John's face.

"It was an accident. We were playing hide and seek near here. Josh had followed his brother Matt. We were quite a bit older than him, but the little bugger was always sticking around. A real drag. He had his dog, Wawa, with him. It looked like an ugly rat."

"Don't talk about my dog like that!" Josh protested.

"You want me to tell them what happened? Then shut up! At one point, when it was time to hide again, Matt left Josh behind, and the snotty-nosed kid and his barking rat stuck with me."

Toby paused. He cried in silence.

"What happened next?" I asked.

"I pushed him. In the dark, I didn't see we were on the edge of a ravine."

"Why did you push him?" Alex asked.

"I wanted him to get away from me, to leave me alone, but he lost his footing. He grabbed me, and we both fell into the stream. He hit his head on a rock. By the time I realized what had happened . . . in the dark . . . he had drowned."

He fell silent.

"What did you do next?" I asked after a moment.

"I panicked. I hid the body in the bushes."

"Why hide the body if it was an accident?"

"Because no one would have believed me."

"What makes you think that?" Alex asked.

"Because I'd been involved in 'accidents' before."

"What kinds of accidents?" I asked.

"Like the time my sister found her cat dead in the barn. Or the time when our neighbour lost . . ."

"Okay, it's okay!" I said. "We don't need to know everything."

"You mean those were not accidents," Alex said.

"No. But with Josh, it was a real accident, and I knew my parents wouldn't believe me. My father was already hitting me hard for no reason, so imagine what he'd have done to me. That's why I decided to cover up the accident.

I put Josh's body in the brushes, and since Wawa was barking like crazy, I didn't have any other choice but to . . ."

Josh was in tears, holding onto his dog.

After a short pause, Toby told us the rest of the story.

"I told the police where to look. I sent them beside the cemetery, away from the stream. It was plausible that Josh had gone and hidden near the graveyard. He could have been kidnapped by a maniac. The search lasted for days. When they finally quit, I fetched the bodies and put them in an old wooden trunk."

"What did you do with the trunk?" I asked.

"I buried it."

"Where?"

He took some time before answering my question.

"In the basement."

"In what basement?" Alex asked.

Toby glanced at her like she was the dumbest person on earth.

"Wake up, snooper. You're not very bright, are you?"

"In the school's basement," I said. "Josh's body is here, underneath our feet."

"Bingo, Einstein!"

"What did you do afterward?" I asked.

"I did the only thing I could do. I shut my mouth, and I took my secret to my grave."

"How did you die?" Alex said.

"Car accident. Not far from here."

"How long ago?"

"Happened in '84."

"In '84!? We weren't even born then!"

"What about Josh's accident?" I asked. "When did it happen?"

"In '66."

"What!?"

"Oh, my God!" Alex exclaimed. "In 1966, even my mother wasn't born!"

"Toby, do you realize that by hiding Josh's accidental death, you made him your prisoner?" I asked.

"I became a prisoner too. Prisoner of my secret. Until the end of my life, I tried to forget by using all kinds of substances, so much so that people started calling me 'Hangover.' My life became an endless hangover. A hellish life."

As soon as Toby was done telling his story, John's body collapsed to the floor. Shortly afterward, a ball of grey light emerged from it and floated above it. Alex made a move toward it, but I stopped her. The ball became translucent, and then a swarm of moths came out of it. They flew in circles around the classroom before escaping through a window.

The ball of light followed the moths. Once outside, it stopped and hovered in front of the school for a little while before taking the shape of the face I had seen earlier when I opened my eyes. Toby's face.

"You can leave now," I shouted. "You no longer need to stay here to protect your secret."

As soon as I said that, the face disappeared into the night.

Shortly afterward, John regained consciousness. He looked rather shaken.

"John, are you all right?"

"What happened?" He looked at Alex. "Why is there blood on your face?"

"You've been possessed," Alex replied. "You hit me with a bungee cord."

"Possessed? I hit you? You're kidding me!"

"She's telling the truth. You don't remember anything?"

"No. I felt something . . . like, getting inside me, and I lost it. It was like I'd been shoved inside a closet, gagged, blindfolded, and my ears plugged. It was a very weird feeling."

While John was describing his experience, Josh's ghost came toward me. It looked different, almost as if it were made of flesh and bone. He was smiling, and his dog was frantically licking his face.

"Let's go down to the basement," he said.

He went down first, and I followed.

I can't believe I'm telling a story like this. I followed a ghost. Yeah.

The basement was dimly lit by the first light of dawn. Josh's ghost stopped in front of the wooden box where a few logs remained.

"Toby buried the trunk underneath this box."

Josh looked at us, one by one, waved his small hand, and vanished with his dog.

"Mission accomplished, Josh," I said.

"We'll never forget you," Alex said.

"Good riddance!" John exclaimed.

"John!"

"What? You're not the one that's been possessed. By the way, what happened to my hand? It hurts like hell, and it's all swollen."

I took the shovel from behind the furnace and started digging while telling John what had happened during his blackout.

"And this is where Josh's body is supposed to be?" John said.

"And his dog's, too," Alex added.

The dirt floor was as hard as cement. John would have liked to help, but he couldn't because of his hand. Alex did her share and I must say that she impressed me, but I am the one who got to shovel the last pieces of dirt before hitting something solid.

The trunk was indeed there. Alex and I dragged it out

with caution because the wood was quite rotten. I hit the lock twice with the shovel to break it open. When I lifted the lid, I was shaking so much that I got a splinter in my thumb. I quickly forgot the pain when I smelled the foul odour emanating from the trunk. Man! It was the same stench we'd smelled the night before but multiplied by ten. I closed the lid.

"Hold your breath," I said.

I took a deep breath as if I were going to go under-water and reopened the trunk. And there we saw, side by side, a small skeleton the size of a child and the remains of an animal wrapped in a blue windbreaker.

"Josh. Wawa. You can rest in peace now."

What else could I say? I closed the trunk, and we collected ourselves for a moment. After that, we went outside. The air was cool and the sun was rising.

HEADLINES

onday morning, our discovery made the headlines.

Human Remains Discovered
Near Spiritwood, Saskatchewan

REGINA, Canadian Press

On Sunday morning, three teenagers found human remains in the basement of an abandoned country school near Spiritwood, in northern Saskatchewan, the RCMP announced today.

The identity of the body has not yet been formally established by the RCMP, but local residents say it could be the remains of Josh Vicente, a nine-year-old boy who disappeared on June 28, 1966. The Vicente family has been contacted by police in an effort to gather a DNA sample for analysis.

Meanwhile, the body has been transported to the RCMP forensic laboratory in Edmonton.

Matthew Vicente, one of the boy's older brothers, as well as his mother, Maria Vicente, said it would be a tremendous relief for the family if the identification was positive.

Police have scheduled a press conference at 3 p.m. tomorrow to provide more information about the circumstances that led to the grim discovery.

As for the three teenagers who found the remains, the RCMP announced that their identities will not be revealed. According to police, they were badly shaken by the discovery and requested anonymity.

FINAL WORDS

I am skipping the details of the police interrogation, the deposition, and the rest. I am also skipping the details of the reunion with my mom. I'll simply say that if she dies prematurely, it will be my fault.

On the Sunday night, after getting back home, my mom made me an enormous bowl of spaghetti with her meatball sauce that I love so much. Real comfort food!

That night, I dreamed of Josh. The dream didn't take place in the Spiritwood school, but in my bedroom, at home.

In the dream, I opened my eyes and saw Josh standing beside my bed. He looked transformed. With his eyes twinkling, he was smiling at me. "I came to say thank you. Thanks to you, I'm free at last, and my family will finally get closure."

"You don't need to thank me, I only did what I knew I ought to."

"If you knew how many people turned a blind eye, ignoring my cry for help . . ."

"I don't understand how someone could do such a thing."

"You know, Ethan, not everyone is as perceptive as you are. It's a gift."

I asked him what he meant.

"Only a few people have an open mind and the sensitivity required to pick up messages from beyond. You saw it with your friends."

"You mean Reggie and Britney?"

"Yes. Those two are deaf and blind when it comes to the other side."

So that was it. He'd confirmed what I'd thought all along.

I couldn't help but ask him the question that was bugging me. "Is the legend of the northern lights true?"

Josh started laughing. "What do you think?" He winked at me and disappeared.

On my way back from Spiritwood, I made a vow to myself to burn my whistle in order to never conjure up spirits again, but after that dream, I changed my mind.

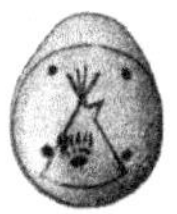

TV stations broadcast a news report in which they showed pictures of Josh. It was indeed the boy I'd seen in the school near Spiritwood and in my dream. One reporter interviewed Josh's mother. She mentioned that she was hoping to get a chance to thank in person the people who gave her back her son. I may sound heartless, but I have no intention of meeting her.

It may sound cool, even heroic, to discover the remains of a missing person, but it's not at all. Since it happened, I've had nightmares, which rarely happened before. I had one again last night in which I was surrounded by spaghetti monsters, and Toby's face was suspended in mid-air, blowing his freezing breath on me. Not cool at all, I tell you.

In one newscast, Josh's mom mentioned that she'd received flowers every year on Mother's Day until 1984: a small bouquet with a card that said, *I love you, Mom. J.* She showed one of those cards on camera. The poor woman said that year after year, the reminder of her son's unexplained disappearance brought up another bout of depression. I have a good idea who was playing that cruel game.

I've done a bit of research on Toby. There was, in fact, a Toby R (I won't write his whole name, just in case) who was killed in a car crash near Spiritwood in 1984, like the ghost told us. What he didn't mention, though, is that he was driving under the influence and that there were two more victims in the crash: his wife and his son.

I got back to Regina last night after spending the summer with my dad in Winnipeg. Can't say it was fantastic, but at least it gave me time to write my story.

I haven't heard from Britney or Reggie. No call, no text, nothing. John was telling me this morning that Reg has changed since he started dating Brit. Hard to believe that he can be even more of an ass than he was before.

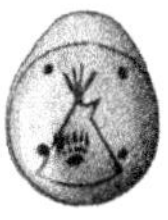

I just got back from Wascana Park. I walked around the lake with Alex. It was great to see the lake again. And to see her. She calls us "ghost rescuers." She's funny. I'd heard about ghostbusters before, but never rescuers.

She suggested that we should go visit Fort San, the old, abandoned sanatorium down in the Qu'Appelle Valley.

Apparently, the place is haunted. I don't really feel like it right now, but who knows, maybe next summer.

Now that I've put my story on paper, I'm anxious to see if it will help me make sense of the events. I certainly hope so because it's been a heck of a job to write all this down, but I didn't mind it after all.

Ethan

THE INSPIRATION

The Ghosts of Spiritwood stems from ideas generated during a series of six writing workshops held with the Grade 8 French immersion students at Elsie Mironuck School in Regina, in 2009 and 2010.

Thank you to teacher Mario Lévesque and his students: Shanine Amin, Jennifer Amundson, Holly Atkinson, Tyra Bear, Benjamin Bodnarchuk, Malachi Costley, Nicole Diewold, Alexis Fellner, Hayley Gibson, Chanel Hanson, Meshal Javid, Chase Kirk, Arizona Lagimodiere, Cassendra Larsen, Dierdre Larsen, Jae-Lee Looker, Mackenzie Looker, Keira Meisner, Joseph Miller, Jadin Murray, Gabrielle Mushanski, Michael Outerbridge, Sydney Patel, Tobiah Picard, Katherine Psoika, Elizabeth Quinn, Leah Rein, Carter Rothecker, Samantha Safinuk,

Autumn Schaefer, Austin Schlosser, Daniel Sudom, Matthew Sudom and Gauge Watchan.

ABOUT THE AUTHOR

Photo by Tim Maw

Born and raised in Québec, Martine Noël-Maw has called Saskatchewan home since 1993. A French literature graduate from the Université de Montréal, she has authored sixteen books and a number of plays for both adults and youth. Her work has earned her many honours, including two Saskatchewan Book Awards and a SATAward. She was longlisted for the *Prix de la nouvelle Radio-Canada* (French CBC Short Story Prize) and shortlisted for the *Prix du récit Radio-Canada* (French CBC Nonfiction Prize). Martine is also an editor, publisher, and translator. Find her online at martinenoelmaw.wordpress.com.

ALSO BY MARTINE NOËL-MAW

Laïka, où es-tu?, youth novel, La nouvelle plume, Regina, 2023

Will & Ernest, théâtre/drama, French and English, La nouvelle plume, Regina, 2020

Le chêne et le papillon, conte, La nouvelle plume, Regina, 2018

Regarde derrière toi!, youth novel, La nouvelle plume, 2018

Trois millions de pas, young adult novel, Hurtubise, 2014

Louis Riel, combattant métis, a biography for youth, Éditions de l'Isatis, 2014

Le 13e souhait, youth novel, La nouvelle plume, 2013

Chemin faisant, La légende des 4, Collection of plays, La nouvelle plume, 2012

Les fantômes de Spiritwood, youth novel, La nouvelle plume, 2010

Le trésor du Wascana, youth novel, La nouvelle plume, 2009

Dans le pli des collines, 2e édition, novel, La nouvelle plume, 2009

Les perles de Ludivine, youth novel, Hurtubise, 2008

Drôle-de-zèbre, youth novel, La nouvelle plume, 2007

La malchance d'Austin, youth novel, La nouvelle plume, 2007

Amélia et les papillons, youth novel, Hurtubise, 2006

Dans le pli des collines, novel, La nouvelle plume, 2004

IN ENGLISH

In the Fold of the Hills, translation of *Dans le pli des collines* by
Margaret Wilson Fuller, Ekstasis Editions, 2013

ALSO FROM SHADOWPAW PRESS

New books by established and emerging authors

Thickwood by Gayle M. Smith

The Emir's Falcon by Matt Hughes

One Lucky Devil by Sampson J. Goodfellow

The Headmasters by Mark Morton

The Good Soldier by Niv Yaniv

The Traitor's Son by Dave Duncan

Paths to the Stars by Edward Willett

Shapers of Worlds

Shapers of Worlds Volume II

Shapers of Worlds Volume III

Shapers of Worlds Volume IV

Star Song by Edward Willett

Dollybird by Anne Lazurko

Small Reckonings by Karin Melberg Schwier

Canadian Chills

Return of the Grudstone Ghosts

Ghost Hotel

Invasion of the IQ Snatchers

by Arthur Slade

Let Us Be True by Erna Buffie